0100498

P9-DGK-946

0 1021 0134873 2

ON LINE

A Michael Neugebauer Book

NORTH-SOUTH BOOKS / NEW YORK / LONDON

LITTLE RED CAP

The Brothers Grimm / Illustrated by Lisbeth Zwerger
Translated from the German by Elizabeth D. Crawford

Once there was a sweet little girl, beloved by everyone who laid eyes on her, but most of all by her grandmother, who couldn't do enough for the child. One time the grandmother gave her a little cap of red silk, and because it pleased her so much and she wore it all the time, she was known as Little Red Cap.

One day her mother said to her, "Come, Little Red Cap, here's a cake and a bottle of wine to take to your grandmother. She is ill and weak, and they will be a treat for her. Now go along before it gets hot, and be sure to walk carefully and don't stray from the path. Otherwise, you may fall and break the bottle, and then Grandmother will have nothing. And when you go into her room, don't forget to say good-day, and don't stare at every corner first." "I will do everything right," said Little Red Cap, and she gave her mother her word on it.

The grandmother lived out in the forest, half an hour from the village.
As Little Red Cap went into the forest, she was met by a wolf. Little Red Cap
didn't know what a bad animal he was, and she was not afraid of him.

"Good-day, Little Red Cap," he said.

"Thank you, Wolf."

"Where are you off to so early, Little Red Cap?"

"To Grandmother's."

"What are you carrying in your basket?"

"Cake and wine. We baked yesterday so I can take a treat to my grandmother.
She is ill and weak, and they will strengthen her."

"Where does your grandmother live, Little Red Cap?"

"A good quarter of an hour into the forest. Her house is the one under three big
oak trees. There are hazelnut bushes around it. That's how you know it,"
said Little Red Cap.

The wolf thought to himself, This tender young thing is a tasty morsel that will go down even better than the old lady. If you manage things very carefully, perhaps you can catch them both.

He strolled along beside Little Red Cap for a bit, then said, "Little Red Cap, just see all the pretty flowers growing around here. Why don't you look about you? I don't think you even hear how beautifully the birds are singing. You're walking as if you were going to school, and it's so much fun out in the forest."

Little Red Cap opened her eyes. When she saw how the sunbeams danced back and forth through the trees and the beautiful flowers that grew everywhere, she thought, If I were to bring Grandmother a fresh bouquet, it would make her happy. It's so early in the day that I'll still get there in time.

And she ran off the path into the forest and began gathering flowers. When she had picked one, she saw that farther on there was an even prettier one and ran to it, and so she went deeper and deeper into the forest.

The wolf, however, went straight to the grandmother's house and knocked
on the door.

"Who's there?"

"Little Red Cap, bringing you cake and wine. Open the door."

"Just press the latch," called the grandmother. "I am too weak and
cannot get up."

The wolf pressed the latch, the door sprang open, and without a word he
went right to the grandmother's bed and gobbled her up. Then he put on her
clothes, set her cap on his head, laid himself in her bed, and drew the curtains.

Meanwhile, Little Red Cap had run everywhere after flowers. When she had so many that she could carry no more, she remembered her grandmother and went on her way to her. She wondered at the door standing open, and as she walked into the room, everything seemed strange to her. Oh my goodness, she thought, how uneasy I am today! And usually I'm so happy at Grandmother's.

"Good-day, Grandmother!" she called out, but received no answer. Then she went to the bed and pulled back the curtains. There lay her grandmother, her cap pulled down over her face, looking very strange.

"Oh, Grandmother, what big ears you have!"
"That's so I can hear you better."
"Oh, Grandmother, what big eyes you have!"
"That's so I can see you better."
"Oh, Grandmother, what big hands you have!"
"That's so I can hold you better."
"Oh, Grandmother, what a dreadfully big mouth you have!"
"That's so I can eat you better!"

And with these words, the wolf sprang out of bed and swallowed up poor Little Red Cap.

Now that he had stilled his appetite, the wolf lay down in the bed again, fell asleep, and began to snore loudly.

A hunter was just passing the house and thought, How the old lady snores! You had better see if something is wrong with her. So he walked into the room, and when he came to the bed, he saw that the wolf was lying in it.

"Here you are, you old sinner," he said. "I've been looking for you."

He was about to aim his rifle, when the thought occured to him that the wolf could have eaten the old lady and she might still be saved. He didn't shoot but took scissors and began to cut open the belly of the sleeping wolf.

When he had made a few snips, he saw the red cap gleaming. After a few more snips, the girl jumped out and cried, "Oh, how frightened I was! How dark it was in the wolf's body!" And then out came the grandmother, also still alive but scarcely able to breathe.

Little Red Cap quickly fetched some large stones, with which they filled the wolf's body. When he woke up, he tried to run away, but the stones were so heavy that he fell down dead.

How all three celebrated! The hunter took the skin off the wolf and went home with it. The grandmother ate the cake and drank the wine that Little Red Cap had brought her and recovered.

But Little Red Cap said to herself, "Never again in your life will you wander alone off the path into the forest when your mother has told you not to."

First North-South Books edition published in 1995.
Copyright © 1983 by Michael Neugebauer Verlag AG, Gossau Zurich, Switzerland
First published in German under the title ROTKÄPPCHEN
English translation is used with the kind permission of William Morrow & Company, New York.

Distributed in the United States by North-South Books Inc., New York

Library of Congress Cataloging in Publication Data
Little Red Riding Hood. Little Red Cap.
Summary: A little girl is eaten by a wolf who masquerades as her sick grandmother.
[1. Fairy tales. 2. Folklore—Germany.] I. Grimm, Jacob, 1785-1863. Rotkäppchen.
II. Zwerger, Lisbeth, ill. III. Title.
PZ8.L733 1983   398.2'1'0943 82-14211
ISBN 1-55858-382-3 (trade edition)
ISBN 1-55858-430-7 (paperback)

British Library Cataloguing in Publication Data is available

TR 10 9 8 7 6 5 4 3 2 1
PB 10 9 8 7 6 5 4 3 2 1
Printed in Italy